Noah and His Wagon written by Jerry Ruff and illustrated by Katrijn Jacobs

ISBN 978-1-60537-710-0

This book was printed in June 2022 at Nikara, M. R. Štefánika 858/25, 963 01 Krupina, Slovakia.

First Edition
10 9 8 7 6 5 4 3 2 1

Clavis Publishing supports the First Amendment and celebrates the right to read.

Noah and His Wagon

Written by Jerry Ruff
Illustrated by Katrijn Jacobs

Clavis

NEW YORK

When Paloma's best friend, Emily Rose, moved away,
the sky grew heavy, and the days became long and dull.
Now there was only Mamá, Paloma's dog Bucket,
and her sitter Jasmine, who was boring and
never got off her phone.

At night Paloma would stare out her bedroom window at the dark. When it rained, she would listen for faraway thunder—faraway like Emily Rose. When her eyes grew tired, she would pull Bucket close and pray for Emily Rose to come back.

Then, her heart heavy, she would drift into sleep.

On weekday mornings,
Jasmine came to Paloma's house.
Today was Monday.
Paloma was finishing her cereal.

Mamá said to Jasmine,
"There's cold chicken and fruit salad for lunch.
Bucket needs to go out again. If it rains,
close the windows. I gotta go—*adiós.*"

Mamá kissed Paloma and took a final sip
of coffee before heading out the door.
Paloma put her bowl in the sink.
Then, she got dressed, brushed her teeth,
combed her hair, and found Bucket's leash.

Paloma, Jasmine, and Bucket went for a walk.
"That dog has to stop at every tree!"
Jasmine complained. Looking at her phone,
she didn't see that Bucket hadn't stopped at a tree.

Instead, he was wagging his tail at a boy with
dark hair, soft eyes, and a little hat on his head.
The boy was coming up the sidewalk.
Behind him, he pulled a wagon.

"*Hola*," said Paloma to the boy.

In the boy's wagon, a grey cat curled up on a blanket.

"Is that your cat?" Paloma asked.

"Hello," said the boy. "Yes, that's Mitzvah.

Does your dog want to ride?"

"Dogs and cats don't mix," said Jasmine.

She looked up from her phone to see who was talking.

"Who are you?" she asked.

"I'm Noah," said the boy.

Then Bucket jumped into the wagon.

After giving Mitzvah a hello sniff,

Bucket curled up and went to sleep too.

"Well, I'll be," said Jasmine.

"What kind of name is *Mitzvah*?" Paloma asked.

"It's Hebrew," Noah said.

"It means 'commandment.'

Like to do something good.

What kind of name is *Bucket*?"

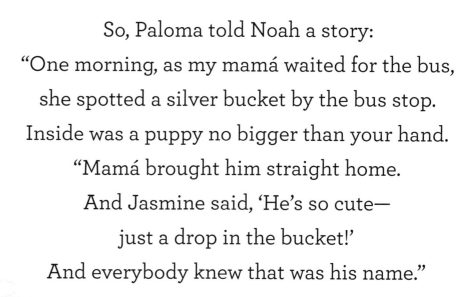

So, Paloma told Noah a story:

"One morning, as my mamá waited for the bus,

she spotted a silver bucket by the bus stop.

Inside was a puppy no bigger than your hand.

"Mamá brought him straight home.

And Jasmine said, 'He's so cute—

just a drop in the bucket!'

And everybody knew that was his name."

Jasmine smiled proudly at the story.

"You're new around here, aren't you?" she said to the boy.

"We moved into the green house last month," Noah said.

"What's that on your head?" Paloma asked.

"It's a *kippah*," the boy told her. "You want to go to the park?"

Jasmine looked at the cloudy sky. A slight breeze carried the smell of rain.

But Jasmine and Paloma followed Noah and his wagon anyway.

Up ahead, an old woman with skinny arms and
large shoes carried heavy bags of groceries.
Every few steps, the woman would stop, put the bags on the ground,
and shake her arms like a wet bird.

"That's Mrs. Willow," Noah said.

"You know her?" asked Paloma.

She had seen the woman before, but didn't know her name or where she lived.

"Her husband died," Noah said. "She walks to the grocery store once a week.
She doesn't have a car."

"How do you know all that? You just moved here," Jasmine said.

"I have a wagon," said Noah.

Noah put the groceries in the wagon alongside Mitzvah and Bucket.

"You're the picture of kindness," Mrs. Willow said to Noah.

"It's going to rain," said Noah. "How are your cats?"

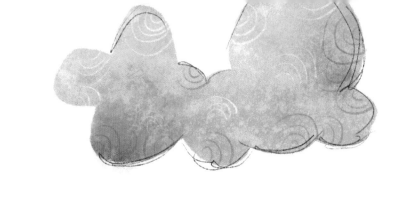

They continued toward the park.

There, a mother was pushing a little boy on a swing.

Another boy sat on the edge of a sandbox. His face wore a scowl.

"Hey, it's Noah and his wagon!" shouted the boy on the swing.

"Hi, Seymour!" called Noah.

The boy in the sandbox looked up. He looked at Noah,
and Paloma, and Jasmine. He looked at Mrs. Willow.
His face didn't grow brighter.
"I have cookies in the bag," said Mrs. Willow.
"It's time for a cookie break. You want to join us, Mikhail?"

They took the blanket from Noah's wagon and spread it on the grass. Everyone sat down—Mikhail too—and Mrs. Willow took out a box of cookies.

Paloma chewed her last bite of cookie as the first raindrop fell. "Time to head home," said Mrs. Willow.

As Paloma lay in bed that night,
she listened to the rain. She thought of Emily Rose.
She thought of Mrs. Willow, and Seymour, and Mikhail.
She thought of Jasmine and Mamá.
She thought of Bucket and Mitzvah.
And she thought of Noah and his wagon.
She patted Bucket gently.
She listened to the rain.
She didn't feel alone.
And soon she was asleep.